MW01035463

Antonio Tabucchi

The Woman
of Porto Pim

Translated from the Italian
by Tim Parks

archipelago books

Copyright © Antonio Tabucchi, 2013
English language translation © Tim Parks, 1991

First Archipelago Books Edition, 2013

All rights reserved. No part of this book may be reproduced or transmitted
in any form without the prior written permission of the publisher.

First published as *Donna di Porto Pim* by Sellerio editore in 1983.

Archipelago Books
232 3rd Street #A111
Brooklyn, NY 11215
www.archipelagobooks.org

Library of Congress Cataloging-in-Publication Data
Tabucchi, Antonio, 1943–2012.
[Donna di Porto Pim. English]
The woman of Porto Pim / Antonio Tabucchi ; translated from the Italian
by Tim Parks. – 1st Archipelago Books ed.
p. cm.
ISBN 978-1-935744-74-0
1. Whales – Fiction. 2. Whaling – Fiction.
3. Short stories, Italian – Translations into English. I. Parks, Tim. II. Title.
PQ4880.A24D6613 2012
853'.914—dc22   2012025599

Cover art: Henri Michaux

The publication of *The Woman of Porto Pim* was made possible with support from
Lannan Foundation, the National Endowment for the Arts, and the New York
State Council on the Arts, a state agency.

Contents

Prologue

I am very fond of honest travel books and have always read plenty of them. They have the virtue of bringing an *elsewhere*, at once theoretical and plausible, to our inescapable, unyielding *here*. Yet an elementary sense of loyalty obliges me to put any reader who imagines that this little book contains a travel diary on his or her guard. The travel diary requires either a flair for on-the-spot writing or a memory untainted by the imagination that memory itself generates – qualities which, out of a paradoxical sense of realism, I have given up any hope of acquiring. Having reached an age at which it seems more dignified to cultivate illusions than foolish aspirations, I have resigned myself to the destiny of writing after my own fashion.

Having said this, it would nevertheless be dishonest to

pass these pages off as pure fiction: the friendly, I might almost say pocket-size muse that dictated them could not even remotely be compared with the majestic muse of Raymond Roussel, who managed to write his *Impressions d'Afrique* without ever stepping off his yacht. I did step off and put my feet on the ground, so that as well as being the product of my readiness to tell untruths, this little book partly has its origins in the time I spent in the Azores. Basically, its subject matter is the whale, an animal which more than any other would seem to be a metaphor; and shipwrecks, which insofar as they are understood as failures and inconclusive adventures, would likewise appear to be metaphorical. My respect for the imaginations which conjured up Jonah and Captain Ahab has luckily saved me from any attempt to sneak myself, via literature, in amongst the ghosts and myths that inhabit our imaginations. If I talk about whales and shipwrecks, it is merely because in the Azores such phenomena can boast an unequivocal reality. There are however two stories in this small volume which it would not be entirely inappropriate to define as fiction. The first, in its basic outline, is the life of Antero de Quental, that great and unhappy poet who measured the depths of the universe and the human spirit within the brief compass of the sonnet. I owe to Octavio Paz's suggestion that poets have no biography and that their work is their biography, the idea of writing this story as if its subject were a fictional character. And then lives lost by the wayside, like Antero's, perhaps hold up better than others to being told along the lines of the hypothetical. The story which closes the book, on the other hand, I owe to the confidences of a man whom I may be supposed to have met in a tavern in Porto Pim. I won't rule out my having altered it with the kind of additions and motives typical of one who believes that he can draw out the sense of a life just by telling its story. Perhaps it will be considered an extenuating circumstance if I confess that alcoholic beverages were consumed in abundance in this tavern and that I felt it would have been impolite of me not to participate in the locally recognised custom.

The fragment of a story entitled "Small Blue Whales Strolling about the Azores" can be thought of as guided fiction, in the sense that it was prompted by a snatch of conversation overheard by chance. I don't even know myself what had happened before and what afterwards. I presume it is about a kind of shipwreck, which is why I put it in the chapter where it is.

The piece entitled "A Dream in Letter Form" I owe partly to reading Plato and partly to the rolling motion of a slow bus from Horta to Almoxarife. It may be that in the transition from dream to text the content has suffered some distortions, but each of us has the right to treat his dreams as he thinks fit. On the other hand the pages entitled "High Seas" aspire to no more than a factual account, the only merit they can claim being their trustworthiness. Similarly many other pages, and I feel it would be superfluous to say which, are mere transcripts of the real or of what others have written before me. Finally, the piece entitled "A Whale's View of Man," in addition to my old vice of looking at things from another's point of view, unashamedly takes its inspiration from a poem by Carlos Drummond de Andrade, who, before myself, and better than myself, chose to see mankind through the sorrowful eyes of a slow animal. And it is to Drummond that this piece is humbly dedicated, partly in memory of an afternoon in Plinio Doyle's house in Ipanema when he told me about his childhood and about Halley's comet.

Vecchiano, 23 September 1982

The Woman
of Porto Pim

Hesperides

A Dream in Letter Form

Having sailed for many days and many nights, I realized that the West has no end, but moves along with us, we can follow it as long as we like without ever reaching it. Such is the unknown sea beyond the Pillars, endless and always the same, and it is from that sea, like the thin backbone of an extinct colossus, that these small island crests rise up, knots of rock lost in the blue.

Seen from the sea, the first island you come to is a green expanse amidst which fruit gleams like gems, though sometimes what you may be seeing are strange birds with purple plumage. The coastline is impervious, black rock-faces inhabited by marauding sea birds which wail as twilight falls, flapping restlessly with an air of sinister torment. Rains are heavy and the sun pitiless: and because of this climate together with the island's rich black soil, the trees are extremely tall, the woods luxuriant and flowers abound, great blue and pink flowers, fleshy as fruit, such as I have never seen anywhere else. The other islands are rockier, though always rich in flowers and fruit, and the inhabitants get much of their food from the woods, and then the rest from the sea, since the water is warm and teeming with fish.

The men have light complexions and astonished eyes, as if the wonder at a sight once seen but now forgotten still played across their faces. They are silent and solitary but not sad and they will frequently laugh over nothing, like children. The women are handsome and proud, with prominent cheekbones and high foreheads. They walk with waterjugs on their heads, and descending the steep flights of steps that lead to the water their bodies don't sway at all, so that they look like statues on which some god has bestowed the gift of movement. These people have no king, they know nothing of class or caste. There are no warriors because they have no need to wage war, having no neighbors. They do have priests, though of a special kind which I will tell you about later on. And anybody can become one, even the humblest peasant or beggar. Their Pantheon is not made up of gods like ours who preside over the sky, the earth, the sea, the underworld, the woods, the harvest, war and peace and the affairs of mankind. Instead they are gods of the spirit, of sentiments and passions. The principal deities are nine in number, like the islands in the archipelago, and each has his temple on a different island.

The god of Regret and Nostalgia is a child with an old man's face. His temple stands on the remotest of the islands in a valley protected by impenetrable mountains, near a lake, in a desolate, wild stretch of country. The valley is forever covered by a light mist, like a veil; there are tall beech trees which whisper in the breeze; a place of intense melancholy. To reach the temple you have to follow a path cut into the rock like the bed of a dried stream. And as you walk you come across strange skeletons of enormous unknown animals, fish perhaps, or maybe birds; and seashells, and stones the pink of mother-of-pearl. I called it a temple, but I ought to have said a shack: for the god of Regret and Nostalgia could hardly live in a palace or luxurious villa; instead he has but a hovel, poor as wept tears, something that stands amidst the things of this world with that same sense of shame as some secret sorrow lurking in our hearts. For this god is not only the god of Regret and Nostalgia; his deity extends to an area of the mind that includes remorse, and the sorrow for that which once was and which no longer causes sorrow but only the memory of sorrow, and the sorrow for that which never was but should have been, which is the most consuming sorrow of all. Men go to visit him dressed in wretched sackcloth, women cover themselves with dark cloaks; and they all stand in silence and sometimes you hear weeping, in the night, as the moon casts its silver light over the valley and over the pilgrims stretched out on the grass nursing their lifetime's regrets.

The god of Hatred is a little yellow dog with an emaciated look, and his temple stands on a tiny cone-shaped island: it takes many days and nights of travelling to get there and only real hatred, the hatred that swells the heart unbearably, spawned on envy and jealousy, could prompt the unhappy sufferer to undertake such an arduous voyage. Then there are the gods of Madness and of Pity, the god of Generosity and the god of Selfishness: but I never went to visit these gods and have heard only vague and fanciful stories in their regard.

As for their most important god, who would seem to be father of all the other gods and likewise of the earth and sky, the accounts I heard of him varied greatly, and I wasn't able to see his temple nor to approach his island. Not because foreigners aren't allowed there, but because even the citizens of this republic can go there only after attaining a spiritual state, which is but rarely achieved – and once there they do not come back. On this god's island stands a temple for which the inhabitants of the archipelago have a name I could perhaps translate as "The Marvelous Dwellings." It consists of a city which is entirely suppositional – in the sense that the buildings themselves don't exist; only their plans have been traced out on the ground. This city has the shape of a circular chessboard and stretches away for miles and miles: and every day, using simple pieces of chalk, the pilgrims move the buildings where they choose, as if they were chess pieces; so that the city is mobile and mutable and its physiognomy is constantly changing. From the centre of the chessboard rises a tower on the top of which rests an enormous golden sphere which vaguely recalls the fruit so abundant in the gardens of these islands. And this sphere is the god. I haven't been able to find out who exactly this god might be: the definitions offered me to date have been imprecise and tentative, not easily comprehensible to the foreigner perhaps. I presume that he has something to do with the idea of completeness, of plentitude, of perfection: a highly abstract idea, not easily comprehensible to the human intellect. Which is why I did think this might be the god of Happiness: but the happiness of those who have understood the sense of life so fully that death no longer has any importance for them; and that is why the chosen few who go to honor the god never return. The task of watching over this god has been given to an idiot with a doltish face and garbled speech who is perhaps in touch with divinity in mysterious ways unknown to reason. When I expressed my desire to pay this god homage, people smiled at me and with an air of profound affection, which perhaps contained a hint of compassion, kissed me on both cheeks.

But I did pay homage along with others to the god of Love, whose temple stands on an island with white curving beaches on the bright sand washed by the sea. And the image of this god isn't an idol, nor anything visible, but a sound, the pure sound of sea water drawn into the temple through a channel carved from the rock and then breaking in a secret pool: and because of the shape of the walls and the size of the building, the sound from the pool reproduces itself in an endless echo, ravishing whoever hears it and inducing a sort of intoxication, or daze. And those who worship this god expose themselves to many and strange effects, since his is the principle which commands life, though it is a bizarre and capricious principle; and while it may be true that he is the soul and harmony of the elements, he can also produce illusions, ravings, visions. And on this island I witnessed spectacles that disturbed me in their innocent truth: so much so that I began to doubt whether they weren't rather the ghosts of my own feelings leaving my body to take shape and apparent reality in the air as a result of my exposing myself to the bewitching sound of the god. It was with such thoughts in my mind that I set out along a path that leads to the highest point of the island, whence you can see the sea on every side. At which I became aware that the island was deserted, that there was no temple on the beach and that the figures and faces of love I had seen like *tableaux vivants* and which included numerous gradations of the spirit, such as friendship, tenderness, gratitude, pride and vanity, all these aspects of love I thought I had seen in human form, were just mirages prompted by I don't know what enchantment. And thus I arrived right at the top of the promontory and as, observing the endless sea, I was already abandoning myself to the dejection that comes with disillusion, a blue cloud descended on me and carried me off in a dream: and I dreamed that I was writing you this letter, and that I was not the Greek who set sail to find the West and never came back, but was only dreaming of him.

I

Shipwrecks, Flotsam, Crossings, Distances

Small Blue Whales Strolling about the Azores

Fragment of a Story

She owes me everything, said the man heatedly, everything: her money, her success. I did it for her, I shaped her with my own hands, that's what. And as he spoke he looked at his hands, clenching and unclenching his fingers in a strange gesture, as if trying to grasp a shadow.

The small ferry began to change direction and a gust of wind ruffled the woman's hair. Don't talk like that, Marcel, please, she muttered, looking at her shoes. Keep your voice down, people are watching us. She was blonde and wore big sunglasses with delicately tinted lenses. The man's head jerked a little to one side, a sign of annoyance. Who cares, they don't understand, he answered. He tossed the stub of his cigarette into the sea and touched the tip of his nose as if to squash an insect. Lady Macbeth, he said with irony, the great tragic actress. You know the name of the place I found her in? It was called 'La Baguette', and as it happens she wasn't playing Lady Macbeth, you know what she was doing? The woman took off her glasses and wiped them nervously on her T-shirt. Please, Marcel, she said. She was showing off her arse to a bunch of dirty old men, that's what our great tragic actress was doing. Once again he squashed the invisible insect on the tip of his nose. And I still have photographs, he said.

The sailor going round checking tickets stopped in front of them and the woman rummaged in her bag. Ask him how much longer it'll be, said the man. I feel ill, this old bathtub is turning my stomach. The woman did her best to formulate the question in that strange language, and the sailor answered with a smile. About an hour and a half, she translated. The boat stops for two hours and then goes back. She put her glasses on again and adjusted her headscarf. Things aren't always what they seem, she said. What things? he asked. She smiled vaguely. Things, she said. And then went on: I was thinking of Albertine. The man grimaced, apparently impatient. You know what our great tragedian was called when she was at the Baguette? She was called Carole, Carole Don-Don. Nice, eh? He turned towards the sea, a wounded expression on his face, then came out with a small shout: Look! He pointed southwards. The woman turned and looked with him. On the horizon you could see the green cone of the island rising in sharp outline from the water. We're getting near, the man said, pleased now, I don't think it'll take an hour and a half. Then he narrowed his eyes and leaned on the railings. There are rocks too, he added. He moved his arm to the left and pointed to two deep-blue outcrops, like two hats laid on the water. What nasty rocks, he said, they look like cushions. I can't see them, said the woman. There, said Marcel, a little bit more to the left, right in line with my finger, see? He slipped his right arm around the woman's shoulder, keeping his hand pointing in front. Right in the direction of my finger, he repeated.

The ticket collector had sat down on a bench near the railing. He had finished making his rounds and was watching their movements. Maybe he guessed what they were saying, because he went over to them, smiling, and spoke to the woman with an amused expression. She listened attentively, then exclaimed: Noooo!, and she brought a hand to her mouth with a mischievous, childish look, as though suppressing a laugh. What's he say? the man asked, with the slightly stolid expression of someone who can't follow a conversation. The woman gave the ticket collector a look of complicity. Her eyes were laughing and she was very attractive. He says they're not rocks, she said, deliberately holding back what she had learnt. The man looked at her, questioning and perhaps a little annoyed. They're small blue whales strolling about the Azores, she exclaimed, those are the exact words he used. And she at last let out the laugh she'd been holding back, a small, quick, ringing laugh. Suddenly her expression changed and she pushed back the hair the wind had blown across her face. You know at the airport I mistook someone else for you? she said, candidly revealing her association of ideas. He didn't even have the same build as you and he was wearing an extraordinary shirt you'd never put on, not even for Carnival, isn't it odd? The man made a gesture with his hand, butting in: I stayed behind in the hotel, you know, the deadline's getting closer and the script still needs going over. But the woman wouldn't let him interrupt. It must be because I've been thinking about you so much, she went on, and about these islands, the sun. She was speaking in what was almost a whisper now, as if to herself. I've done nothing all this time but think of you. It never stopped raining. I imagined you sitting on a beach. It's been too long, I think. The man took her hand. For me too, he said, but I haven't been to the beach much, the main thing I've been looking at is my typewriter. And then it rains here too, oh yes, you wouldn't believe the rain, how heavy it is. The woman smiled. I haven't even asked you if you managed to do it, and to think, if ideas were worth anything, I'd have written ten plays with trying to imagine yours: tell me what it's like, I'm dying to know. Oh, let's say it's a reworking of Ibsen in a light vein, he said, without disguising a certain enthusiasm – light, but a little bitter too, the way my stuff is, and seen from her point of view. How do you mean? asked the woman. Oh, the man said with conviction, you know the way things are going these days, I thought it would be wise to present it from her point of view, if I want people to take notice, even if that's not why I wrote it, of course. The story's banal in the end, a relationship breaking up, but all stories are banal, what matters is the point of view, and I rescue the woman, she is the real protagonist, he is selfish and mediocre, he doesn't even realize what he's losing, do you get me?

The woman nodded. I think so, she said, I'm not sure. In any case I've been writing some other stuff as well, he went on, these islands are a crushing bore, there's nothing to do to pass the time but write. And then I wanted to try my hand at a different genre. I've been writing fiction all my life. It seems nobler to me, the woman said, or at least more gratuitous, and hence, how can I put it, lighter . . . Oh right, laughed the man, delicacy: *par délicatesse j'ai perdu ma vie*. But there comes a time when you have to have the courage to try your hand at reality, at least the reality of our own lives. And then, listen, people can't get enough of real-life experience, they're tired of the imaginings of novelists of no imagination. Very softly the woman asked: Are they memoirs? Her subdued voice quivered slightly with anxiety. Kind of, he said, but there's no elaboration of interpretation or memory; the bare facts and nothing more: that's what counts. It'll stir things up, said the woman. Let's say people will take notice, he corrected. The woman was silent for a moment, thoughtful. Do you already have a title? she asked. Maybe *Le regard sans école*, he said, what do you think? Sounds witty, she said.

Steering around in a wide curve, the boat began to sail along the coast of the island. Puffs of black smoke with a strong smell of diesel flew out of the funnel and the engine settled into a calm chug, as if enjoying itself. That's why it takes so long, the man said, the landing stage must be on the other side of the island.

You know, Marcel, the woman resumed, as if pursuing an idea of her own, I saw a lot of Albertine this winter. The boat proceeded in small lurches, as if the engine were jamming. They sailed by a little church right on the waterfront and they were so near they could almost make out the faces of the people going in. The bells summoning the faithful to Mass had a jarring sound, as though dragging their feet.

What?! The man chased the invisible insect from the tip of his nose. What on earth do you mean? he said. His face took on an expression of amazement and great disappointment. We kept each other company, she explained. A lot. It's important to keep each other company in life, don't you think? The man stood up and leaned on the railing, then sat on his seat again. But what do you mean, he repeated, have you gone mad? He seemed extremely restless, his legs couldn't keep still. She's an unhappy woman, and a generous one, the woman said, still following her own reasoning, I think she loved you a great deal. The man stretched out his arms in a disconsolate gesture and muttered something incomprehensible. Listen, forget it, he finally said with an effort, anyway, look, we've arrived.

The boat was preparing to dock. At the stern two men in T-shirts were unrolling the mooring cable and shouting to a third man standing on the landing stage watching them with his hands on his hips. A small crowd of relatives had gathered to greet the passengers and were waving. In the front row were two old women with black headscarves and a girl dressed up as though for her first communion hopping on one foot.

And what about the play, the woman suddenly enquired, as if all at once remembering something she had meant to ask, do you have a title for the play? You didn't tell me. Her companion was sorting out some newspapers and a small camera in a bag that bore the logo of an airline company.

I've thought of hundreds and rubbished them all, he said, still bending down over his bag, not one that's really right, you need a witty title for a thing like this but something that sounds really good too. He stood up and a vague expression of hope lit up in his eyes. Why? he asked. Oh nothing, she said, just asking; I was thinking of a possible title, but maybe it's too frivolous, it wouldn't sound right on a serious poster, and then it's got nothing to do with your subject matter, it would sound completely incongruous. Oh come on, he begged, at least you can satisfy my curiosity, maybe it's brilliant. Silly, she said, completely off target.

The passengers crowded around the gangway and Marcel was sucked into the crush. The woman stood apart, holding on to the cable of the railing. I'll wait for you on the wharf, he shouted, without turning, I've got to move with the crowd! He raised an arm above the gaggle of heads, waving his hand. She leaned on the railing and began to gaze at the sea.

Other Fragments

In April 1839 two British citizens disembarked on the island of Flores which, together with Corvo, is the most remote and isolated island of the Azores archipelago. It was curiosity that had brought them there, always an excellent guide. They landed at Santa Cruz, a village situated at the northernmost point of the island and boasting a small natural port which still offers the safest place to land on Flores today. From Santa Cruz they set out to travel, on foot and by litter, around the coast as far as Lajes de Flores, about forty kilometers away, where they wanted to see a church that the Portuguese had built in the seventeenth century. The litter, borne on the shoulders of eight islanders, was made from a ship's sail and judging by the travelers' description would seem to have been little more than a hammock strung between two poles.

Like all the other islands of the archipelago, Flores is volcanic in origin, although unlike São Miguel or Faial, for example, which have white beaches and brilliant green woods, Flores is just one great slab of black lava in the midst of the ocean. Flowers grow well on volcanoes, as Bécquer was to remark; the two Englishmen thus crossed an incredible landscape; a slab of flowering slate which would suddenly open up into fearful chasms, precipices, sheer cliffs falling to the sea. Halfway to their destination they stopped to spend the night in a little fishing village. It was a tiny settlement perched on top of a cliff and the travelers don't mention the name: not out of carelessness, I don't think, since their account is always precise and detailed, but perhaps because it had no name. Most likely it was simply called *Aldeia*, which means "village," and being the only inhabited place for miles around, this general term did perfectly well for a proper name. From a distance it seemed an attractive place with a tidy geometry, as little fishing villages often are. The houses, however, seemed to have bizarre shapes. When they got to the village they realized why. The fronts of almost all the houses had been made with the prows of sailing ships; they had a triangular floor plan, some were made with good hard woods, and the only stone wall was the one that closed the three sides of the triangle. Some of the houses were quite beautiful, the amazed Englishmen tell us, their interiors scarcely looking like houses at all since almost all the furnishings – lanterns, seats, tables and even beds – had been taken from the sea. Many had portholes for windows, and since they looked out over the precipice and the sea below, they gave the impression of being in a sailing ship which has landed on top of a mountain. These houses were built with the remains of the shipwrecks into which over the centuries the rocks of Flores and Corvo had enticed passing ships. The Englishmen were offered hospitality in a house whose façade bore in white letters the legend THE PLYMOUTH BALTIMORE, which perhaps helped them feel almost at home. And indeed they woke up refreshed the following morning and resumed their journey in the sail.

The two travellers were called Joseph and Henry Bullar, and their journey deserves a mention.

In November 1838 a London doctor, Joseph Bullar, having already tried, without success, all the then known treatments for consumption on his brother, Henry, decided, when Henry's condition deteriorated, to make a voyage with him to the island of São Miguel. Despite the distance and its extraordinary isolation, São Miguel, of all Atlantic islands with a warm climate, was the only one which could guarantee regular communications with England. During the orange season, that is from November to May, you could send a letter to England every week and receive a reply after three weeks, since the ship that carried oranges to England also offered a postal service. In those days São Miguel was one enormous orange orchard from coast to coast, with the trees running right down to the shore.

After a fairly rough voyage on the orange ship, the two brothers arrived at Ponta Delgada in December 1838 and stayed in São Miguel until April 1839. One can assume that Henry's health benefited somewhat, since on leaving the main island the two brothers decided to set out in small fishermen's sailing boats to visit the central and western Azores. Their time in the archipelago, and particularly in Faial, Pico and the remote Corvo, produced a splendid travel diary, which once back in London the Bullar brothers published at John van Voorst's printing press in 1841, under the title *A Winter in*

the Azores and a Summer at the Furnas. One reads it today with
admiration and amazement, though when all is said and done
things on the Azores have not changed so very much.

Almas or alminhas: souls and little souls. A cross on a square
stone block with a blue-and-white tile in the middle depicting St Michael. The souls appear on 2 November when St
Michael fishes them out of purgatory with a rope. He needs
a rope for every soul. São Miguel is full of crosses, and hence
of souls who haunt the reefs, the precipices, the lava beaches
where the sea lashes. Late at night or very early in the morning, if you listen carefully you can hear their voices. Confused
wailing, litanies, whispers, which the skeptical or distracted
may easily mistake for the noise of the sea or the crying of the
vultures. Many are the souls of shipwrecked sailors.

The first ships of the Portuguese explorers broke up here, the
pirate ships of Sir Walter Raleigh and the Earl of Cumber-
land, the Spanish fleet of Don Pedro de Valdez, who wanted to
annex the Azores to King Philip's crown. Actually the Spanish
did manage to disembark and their ruin wasn't complete until

the battle of Salga fought on Terceira in 1581. The islanders waited for the Spanish army on top of a hill, then drove herds of crazed bulls down to rout the invaders. Among the Spanish were Cervantes and Lope de Vega, who described the savage battle in a quatrain.

Then came the fashionable shipwrecks which made the headlines in newspapers and magazines. The vicissitudes of rich, bizarre travellers who had themselves photographed on their luxury yachts as they set sail from New York or New Bedford. Platinum blonde curls in the breeze, blazers with gold buttons, silk scarves. The champagne cork pops and the wine froths out of the bottle. One thinks of foxtrots and other dance music. The names of the boats are as whimsical as the lives of their owners: *Ho Ho, Anahita, Banana Split*. Bon voyage, sirs, announces some minor local politician come to cut the mooring line with silver scissors.

The world is on the rocks too, but they don't seem to notice.

At the end of the nineteenth century, Albert I, Prince of Monaco, sailed by these islands on board his *Hirondelle*. It was in these seas that he carried out many of his excellent oceanographic studies, descended into the deepest waters in his pressure suit, catalogued unknown mollusks, strange life-forms with vague, uncertain shapes, fish and seaweeds. He left some very lively pages on the Azores, but what struck me most of all was his description of the death of a sperm whale, a gigantic animal whose doom is as majestic and terrifying as the wreck of a transatlantic liner.

> In order to observe the normal guidelines of the maritime authorities, the whalers move quickly to tow the sperm-whale's carcass out to sea, since its decomposition would otherwise rapidly contaminate the whole surrounding area. It is not an easy task, for although it might seem sufficient to drag the carcass two or three hundred metres from the shore and rely on a favourable current to carry it away, the capricious wind can always bring it back; sometimes the whalers will struggle in vain to be rid of the stinking hulk for days and days. Then if the sea gets rough, the undesirable carrion may well be trapped by the waves beneath inaccessible cliffs whence its heavy stench will for months and months constitute a tor-ment to the inhabitants of the region. Finally, one hot sunny

day, the large intestine, blown up with gas, will explode with a boom, covering the surrounding area with bits of offal which constitute a delicious food for the multicoloured scavenger crabs. Sometimes these sinister creatures arrange to meet for their foul five o'clock tiffin with elegant shrimps which parade their delicate antennae over the enormous cake, always given that the high tide is so kind as to offer the latter a means of transport. But whatever the details, the fact remains that the poor sperm whale proceeds along the road of his ruin from the first wound inflicted on him by man right through to the action of the humble creatures who take him to the completion of that fatal cycle which is the destiny of every living being. The death of a sperm whale is as majestic as the crumbling of a great building, and in the necropolis set up by the whalers in the little bays, the animal's remains pile up like the broken walls of a cathedral.

For a long time I carried around in my memory a phrase of Chateaubriand's: *Inutile phare de la nuit.* I believe I always attributed to these words the power of comfort in disenchantment: as when we attach ourselves to something that turns out to be an *inutile phare de la nuit*, yet nevertheless allows us to do something merely because we believed in its light: the power of illusions. In my memory this phrase was associated with the name of a distant and improbable island: *Île de Pico, inutile phare de la nuit*.

When I was fifteen I read *Les Natchez*, an incongruous, absurd and in its way magnificent book. It was the gift of an uncle who for the whole of his short life cultivated the dream of becoming an actor and who probably loved Chateaubriand for his theatricality and scene painting. The book fascinated me, took my imagination by the hand and drew it with irresistible force through the stage curtains of adventure. I remember some passages of the book by heart and for years I thought that the phrase about the beacon belonged to it. Then it occurred to me to quote the exact passage in this notebook, so I reread *Les Natchez*, but couldn't find my phrase. At first I thought it had escaped me because I had reread the book with the haste of one who is merely looking for a quote. Then I realized that not finding a phrase like this partakes of the most intimate sense of the phrase itself, and this was a consolation for me. I also wondered what part the perhaps unconscious forces of evocation and suggestion generated by this phrase might have played in calling me to an island where there was nothing to attract me. Sometimes the directions we take in our lives can be decided by the combination of a few words.

I need only add that on Pico at night no beacons shone.

Breezy and Rupert invite me onto their boat for a farewell drink. They are leaving in the afternoon, since in order to get away from the island they want to take advantage of the seven o'clock calm, a phenomenon which exists here as elsewhere. Moored opposite the water tanks, the *Amadeus* is blue and white, rocking gently, and it seems impossible to me that such a small boat is capable of crossing oceans.

Rupert has very red hair, freckles, an amusing, Danny Kaye–like face. Perhaps he told me he was Scottish, or perhaps I just think of him as such because of his face. He used to work in a shipping company in London: years and years sitting at a table under electric light, dreaming of the distant ports whence the company's exotic merchandise arrived. So one day he handed in his notice, sold what he had and bought this boat. Or rather, he had it custom-built to the design of a New York boat architect. And when I go below on the *Amadeus* I appreciate it isn't quite the fragile eggshell it seems when you see it from the land. Breezy came with him and they live together on the boat. Welcome to our home, they say, laughing. Breezy has an open, very friendly face, a marvellous smile, and she's wearing a long flowery dress as if preparing for a garden party, not a transatlantic crossing. The interior is furnished with hard woods and warm-colored upholsteries which immediately convey a feeling of comfort and safety. There is a small, well-stocked library. I begin to browse: Melville, of course, and Conrad and Stevenson. But there is Henry James too, and Kipling, Shaw, Wells, *Dubliners*, Somerset Maugham, Forster, Joyce Cary, H. E. Bates. I pick up *The Jacaranda Tree* and inevitably the conversation turns to Brazil. They have only been as far as Fortaleza do Ceará, sailing down the coasts of America. But they are saving Brazil for another trip; first Rupert has to arrange to rent out the *Amadeus* for a small luxury cruise. That's how they live, renting out the boat, and usually Rupert stays on board and sails it. The rest of their life is all their own.

We lift our glasses and drink to their trip. May fair winds follow you, I toast, now and always. Rupert slides back the door of a shelf and slips a tape into the stereo. It is Mozart's Concerto K 271 for piano and orchestra, and only now do I realize why the boat is called *Amadeus*. The shelf contains the complete works of Mozart on tape, catalogued with meticulous care. I think of Rupert and Breezy crossing the seas to the accompaniment of Mozart's tunes and harpsichords, and for me the idea has a strange beauty to it, perhaps because I have always associated music with the idea of terra firma, of the concert hall or a cozy room in the half dark. The music takes on a solemn sound and draws us in. The glasses are empty, we get up and embrace each other. Rupert starts the engine, I climb onto the steps and with a jump am down on the wharf. There's a soft light on the circle of houses which is Porto Pim. *Amadeus* turns in a wide curve and sets off at speed. Breezy is at the helm and Rupert is hoisting the sail. I stand there waving until *Amadeus*, all its sails already unfurled, reaches the open sea.

When sailors stop at Horta it is a custom to leave a drawing with name and date on the wall of the wharf. The wall is a hundred metres long, and drawings of boats, flag colors, numbers and graffiti are all jumbled up one on top of the other. I record one of the many: "Nat, from Brisbane. I go where the wind takes me."

In July 1985, the winds brought Captain Joshua Slocum as far as Horta. Slocum was the first man to sail solo around the world. His yacht was called *Spray* and the impression you get from photographs is of a tub of a boat, clumsy and unstable, better suited for river sailing than a trip around the world. Captain Slocum left some quite beautiful pages on the Azores. I read them in his *Sailing Alone Around the World*, an old old edition, the cover decorated with a festoon of anchors.

The winds also brought the only woman whaler I ever heard of to the Azores. Her name was Miss Elisa Nye. She was seventeen years old, and to reach her maternal grandfather, the naturalist Thomas Hickling, who had invited her to spend a year with him in his house in São Miguel, she thought nothing of boarding a whaler, the *Sylph*, which was travelling under sail from New Bedford to the Western Isles, as the American then called the Azores. Miss Elisa was a bright, enterprising girl, brought up in an American family of frugal and puritan traditions. She wasn't discouraged by life on the whaler and did her best to make herself useful. Her trip lasted from 10 July to 13 August 1847. In her engaging diary, written with freshness and dispatch, she talks of the sea, of old Captain Garner, gruff and fatherly, the dolphins, the sharks and, of course, the whales. In her free time, apart form keeping up her diary, she read the Bible and Byron's *The Corsair*.

Peter's Bar is a café on the dockside at Horta, near the sailing club. It is a cross between a tavern, a meeting point, an information agency and a post office. The whalers go there, but so too do the yachting folks crossing the Atlantic or making other long trips. And since the sailors know that Faial is an obligatory stopover point and that everybody passes through, Peter's has become the forwarding address for precarious and hopeful messages that otherwise would have no destination. On the wooden counter at Peter's the proprietor pins notes, telegrams, letters, which wait for someone to come and claim them. "For Regina, Peter's Bar, Horta, Azores," says an envelope with a Canadian stamp. "Pedro e Pilar Vazquez Cuesta, Peter's Bar, Azores": the letter was mailed in Argentina and has arrived just the same. A slightly yellowed note says: *"Tom, excuse-moi, je suis partie pour le Brésil, je ne pouvais plus rester ici, je devenais folle. Écris-moi, viens, je t'attends. c/o Engenheiro Silveira Martins, Avenida Atlântica 3025, Copacabana. Brigitte."* Another implores: "Notice. To boats bound for Europe. Crew available!!! I am 24, with 26,000 miles of crewing/cruising/cooking experience. If you have room for one more, please leave word below! Carol Shepard."

She's slim, very streamlined, built of top-quality material. She must have been around a great deal. She arrived in this port by chance. But then journeys are a chance. She's called *Nota azzurra*. Mountains of fire, wind and solitude: thus in the sixteenth century did one of the first Portuguese travellers to land here describe the Azores.

Antero de Quental

A Life

Antero was born the last of nine children into a large Azores family which possessed both pastureland and orange orchards, and so grew up amidst the austere and frugal affluence of island landowners. Among his forebears were an astronomer and a mystic, whose portraits, together with that of his grandfather, adorned the walls of a dark sitting room which smelt of camphor. His grandfather had been called André da Ponte de Quental and had suffered exile and prison for having taken part in the first liberal revolution in 1820. So much his father told him, a kind man who loved horses and had fought in the battle of Mindelo against the absolutists.

To keep him company in his early years he had some small

dappled colts and the archaic lullabies of serving women who came down from the mountains of São Miguel, where the villages are built of lava and have names like Caldeiras and Pico do Ferro. He was a calm pale child, with reddish hair and eyes so clear they sometimes seemed transparent. He spent the mornings on the patio of a solid house where the women kept the keys to the cupboards and the windows had curtains made from thick lace. He ran about letting out little whoops of joy and was happy. He was particularly close to his oldest brother, whose singular and bizarre intelligence would for long periods be overshadowed by a silent madness. Together they invented a game called Heaven and Earth, with cobblestones and shells for pieces, playing on a circular checkerboard sketched in the dust.

When the child was of an age to learn, his father called the Portuguese poet Feliciano de Castilho to their house and entrusted him with the boy's education. At the time Castilho was considered a great poet, perhaps because of his versions of Ovid and Goethe and perhaps again because of the misfortune of his blindness, which sometimes conferred on his poetry that prophetic tone beloved of the Romantics. In fact he was a peevish, crusty scholar with a preference for rhetoric and grammar. With him the young Antero learnt Latin, German and metrics. And amidst these studies he reached adolescence.

On the April night of his fifteenth birthday, Antero woke up with a start and felt that he must go down to the sea. It was a calm night with a waxing moon. The whole household was asleep in silence and went down toward the cliffs. He sat on a rock and looked at the sky, trying to imagine what could have prompted him to come here. The sea was calm and breathed as though asleep, and the night was like any other night. Just that he had a great sense of disquiet, of anxiety weighing on his chest. And at that moment he heard a dull bellow rising from the earth and the moon turned blood red and the sea swelled up like an enormous belly to crash down on the rocks. The earth shook and the trees bent under the force of a rushing wind. Antero ran home, bewildered to find the family gathered together on the patio; but the danger was over now and the women's embarrassment at being seen in their nightclothes was already greater than the fright they had suffered. Before going back to bed, Antero took a piece of paper and, unable to control himself, wrote down some words. And as he wrote he became aware that the words were arranging themselves on the page, by themselves almost, in the form and metre of a sonnet: and he dedicated it, in Latin, to the unknown god who was inspiring him. That night he slept soundly and at dawn dreamt that a small monkey with a sad ironic little face was offering him a note. He read the note and discovered a secret no one else had been allowed to know, except the monkey.

He approached manhood. He studied astronomy and geometry, he came under the spell of Laplace's cosmogony, of the idea of a unity of physical forces and a mathematical conception of space. In the evening he wrote descriptions of mysterious, abstract little contrivances, translating into words his ideas of the cosmic machine. By now he had resigned himself to his dreams of the small monkey with the sad ironic little face and was amazed those nights when the creature did not visit him.

When he reached university age he left for Coimbra as family tradition required and announced that the moment had come for him to give up his studies of cosmic laws and dedicate himself to the laws of man. He was now a tall, solid boy with a blond beard that gave him a majestic, almost arrogant look. In Coimbra he discovered love, read Michelet and Proudhon and, instead of studying the laws used to apply the justice of the time, got excited by the idea of a new justice based on the equality and dignity of man. He pursued this idea with the passion he had inherited from his island forebears, but likewise with the reason of the man he was, for he was convinced that justice and equality formed part of the geometry of the world. In the perfect, closed form of the sonnet, he expressed the ardor that possessed him and his eagerness for truth. He left for Paris and became a typesetter, the way someone else might have become a monk, because he wanted to experience physical tiredness and the concreteness of manual tools. After France he went to England and then North America, living in New York and Halifax, so as to get to know the new metropolises man was building and the different ways of life they engendered. By the time he went back to Portugal he had become a socialist. He founded the National Association of Workers, travelled and made converts, lived among the peasants, passed through his own islands with the fiery oratory of the demagogue; he came against the arrogance of the powerful, the flattery of the sly, the cowardliness of servants. He was animated by disdain and wrote sonnets full of sarcasm and fury. He also experienced the betrayal of certain comrades and the ambiguous alchemy of those who manage to combine the common good with their own advantage.

He realized he would have to leave it to others more able than himself to press on with the work he had begun, almost as though that work no longer belonged to him. The time had come for practical men, and he was not practical. This filled him with a sense of desolation, like a child who loses his innocence and suddenly discovers how vulgar the world is. He wasn't even fifty yet and his face was deeply scored. The eyes had sunk into hollows and his beard was going grey. He began to suffer from insomnia and in the rare moments when he did sleep would let out low muffled cries. Sometimes he had the impression his words did not belong to him and often to his surprise he would catch himself talking out loud alone as if he were somebody else talking to himself, Antero. A Parisian doctor diagnosed hysteria and prescribed electric shock therapy. In a note, Antero wrote that he was suffering from "the infinite," and perhaps in his case this was the more plausible explanation. Perhaps he was just tired of this transitory, imperfect form of the ideal and of passion, his yearning now taking him toward another kind of geometrical order. In his writings, the word *nothing* began to appear, seeming to him now the most perfect form of perfection. In his forty-ninth year he returned to his native island.

The morning of 11 September 1891 he left his house in Ponta Delgada, walked quickly down the steep shady road to Igreja Matriz and went into a small shop on the corner that sold arms. He was wearing a black suit and white shirt, his tie fixed with a tiepin made with a shell. The shopkeeper was a friendly, obese man who loved dogs and old prints. A bronze fan turned slowly in the ceiling. The owner showed his customer a beautiful seventeenth-century print he had recently bought depicting a pack of dogs chasing a stag. The old shopkeeper had been a friend of his father's, and Antero remembered how, as a child, the two men had taken him to the Caloura fair, which boasted the best horses in São Miguel. They talked for a long time about dogs and horses, then Antero bought a small revolver with a short barrel. When he left the shop the bell tower of Matriz was striking eleven. He walked slowly along by the sea as far as the harbor office, and stood a long time on the wharf looking out at the clippers. Then he crossed the coast road and walked into the circle of gaunt plane trees around Praça da Esperança. The sun was fierce and everything was white. The *praça* was deserted at that time of day, because of the extreme heat. A sad-looking donkey, tied to a ring on a wall, let its head loll. As he was crossing the square, Antero caught the sound of music. He stopped and turned. In the opposite corner, under the shade of a plane tree, a tramp was playing a barrel organ. The tramp nodded and Antero walked over to him. He was a lean gypsy and he had a monkey on his shoulder. It was a small animal with a sad, ironic little face, wearing a red uniform with gold buttons. Antero recognized the monkey of his dreams and realized who it was. The animal held out its tiny black hand and Antero dropped a coin in it. In exchange the monkey pulled out one of the many slips of colored paper the gypsy kept tucked in the ribbon of his hat and offered it to him. He took it and read it. He crossed the *praça*, the trees, the sparkle of the sea, the gypsy playing his barrel organ. He felt a warm trickle running down his neck. He clicked the drum of the revolver and fired again. At which the gypsy disappeared along with the rest of the scene and the bells of the Matriz began to strike noon.

II

Of Whales and Whalemen

High Seas

Towards the end of the last war an exhausted and perhaps sick whale ran aground on the beach of a small German town, I don't know which. Like the whale, Germany too was exhausted and sick, the town had been destroyed and the people were hungry. The inhabitants of the little town went to the beach to see this giant visitor who lay there in forced and unnatural immobility and breathed. A few days went by, but the whale didn't die. Every day the people went to look at the whale. No one in the town knew how to kill an animal which wasn't an animal but a huge dark, polished cylinder they had previously seen only in illustrations. Until one day someone took a big knife, went up to the whale, carved out a cone of oily flesh and hurried home with it. The whole population began to carve away pieces of the whale. They went at night, in secret, because they were ashamed to be seen, even though they knew everybody was doing the same thing. The whale went on living for many days, despite being riddled with horrific wounds.

My friend Christopher Meckel told me this story some time ago. I thought I had got it out of my mind, but it came back to me all at once when I got off the boat on the island of Pico and there was a dead whale floating near the rocks.

When whales float in the middle of the ocean they look like drifting submarines struck by torpedoes. And in their bellies one imagines a crew of lots of little Jonahs whose radar is out of operation and who have given up trying to contact other Jonahs and are awaiting their deaths with resignation.

I read in a scientific review that whales use ultrasound to communicate with each other. They have extremely fine hearing and can pick up each other's calls hundreds of kilometres away. Once, herds would communicate with each other from the most distant parts of the globe. Usually they were mating calls or other kinds of messages whose meaning we don't understand. Now that the seas are full of mechanical noises and artificial ultrasound, the whale's messages suffer such interference that other whales can no longer pick them up and decipher them. In vain they go on transmitting calls and signals which wander about lost in the depths of the sea.

There is a position whales assume which fishermen describe as the "dead whale" pose. It is almost always the adult and isolated whale which does this. When "dead," the whale appears to have abandoned itself completely to the surface of the sea, rising and falling without any apparent effort, as though in the grip of a deep sleep. Fishermen claim that this phenomenon occurs only on days of intense heat or with dead-calm seas, but the real reasons for the cetaceous catalepsy are unknown.

Whalemen maintain that whales are entirely indifferent to a human presence even when they are copulating, and that they will let people get so close as to be able to touch them. The sex act takes place by pressing belly to belly, as in the human species. Whalemen say that while mating the heads of the pair come out of the water, but naturalists maintain that whales assume a horizontal position and that the vertical position is just a product of the fishermen's imagination.

Our knowledge of the birth of whales and the first moments of their lives is likewise fairly limited. In any event something different from what we know goes on with other marine mammals must happen to prevent the young whale from being drowned or suffocated when the umbilical cord linking it to the mother's vascular system breaks. As it is well known, birth and copulation are the only moments in the lives of other marine mammals when they seem to remember their terrestrial origins. Thus they come ashore only to mate and give birth, staying just long enough for the young to survive the first phases of their life. Of all terrestrial acts, this then should be the last to fade from the physiological memory of the whale, which of all aquatic mammals is the furthest from its terrestrial origins.

No relationship exists between this gentle race of mammals, who like ourselves have red blood and milk, and the monsters of the previous age, horrible abortions of the primordial slime. Far more recent, the whale found cleansed water, an open sea and a peaceful earth. The milk of the sea and its oil abounded; its warm fat, animalized, seethed with extraordinary strength; it wanted to live. These elements fermented together and formed themselves into great giants, *enfants gâtés* of a nature which endowed them with incomparable strength and, more precious yet, fine fire-red blood. For the first time blood appeared on the scene. Here was the true flower of this world. All the creatures with pale, mean, languid, vegetating blood seem utterly without heart when compared to the generous life that boils up in this porpoise whether in anger or in love. The strength of the higher world, its charm, its beauty, is blood . . . But with this magnificent gift nervous sensibility is likewise infinitely increased. One is far more vulnerable, has far more capacity to suffer and to enjoy. Since the whale has absolutely no sense of the hunt, and its sense of smell and hearing are not very highly developed, everything is entrusted to touch. The fat which defends the whale from the cold does not protect it from knocks at all. Finely arranged in six separate tissues, the skin trembles and quivers at every contact.

The tender papillae which cover the whale are the instruments of a most delicate sense of touch. And all this is animated, brought to life by a gush of red blood, which given the massive size of the animal is not even remotely comparable in terms of abundance to the blood of terrestrial mammals. A wounded whale floods the sea in a moment, dyes it red across a huge distance. The blood which we have in drops has been poured into the whale in torrents.

The female carries her young for nine months. Her tasty rather sugary milk has the warm sweetness of a woman's. But since the whale must always forge through the waves, if the udders were located on the breast, the young whale would be constantly exposed to the brunt of the sea; hence they are to be found a little further down, in a more sheltered place, on the belly, whence the young whale was born. And the baby hides away there and takes pleasure in the wave that his mother breaks for him.

Michelet, *La Mer*, page 238

They say that ambergris is formed from the remains of the keratin shells of shellfish that the whale is unable to digest and which accumulate in certain segments of the intestine. But others maintain that it forms as the result of a pathological process, a sort of limited intestinal calculus. Today ambergris is used almost exclusively in the production of luxury perfumes, but in the past it had as many applications as human fantasy could dream up for it: it was used as a propitiatory balsam in religious rites, as an aphrodisiac lotion, and as a sign of religious dedication for Muslim pilgrims visiting the Qa'aba in Mecca. It is said to have been an indispensable aperitif at the banquets of the Mandarins. Milton talks about ambergris in *Paradise Lost*. Shakespeare mentions it too, I don't remember where.

L'amour, chez eux, soumis à des conditions difficiles, veut un lieu de profonde paix. Ainsi que le noble elephant, qui craint les yeux profanes, la baleine n'aime qu'au desert. Le rendez-vous est vers les poles, aux anses solitaires du Groënland, aux brouillards de Behring, sans doute aussi dans la mer tiède qu'on a trouvée près du pole même.

La solitude est grande. C'est un théâtre étrange de mort et de silence pour cette fête de l'ardente vie. Un ours blanc, un phoque, un renard bleu peut-être, témoins respectueux, prudents, observant à distance. Les lustres et girandoles, les miroirs fantastiques, ne manquent pas. Cristaux bleuâtres, pics, aigrettes de glace éblouissante, neiges vierges, ce sont les témoins qui siègent tout autour et regardent.

Ce qui rend cet hymen touchant et grave, c'est qu'il y faut l'expresse

volonté. Ils n'ont pas l'arme tyrannique du requin, ces attaches qui maîtrisent
le plus faible. Au contraire, leurs fourreaux glissants les séparent, les éloignent.
Ils se fuient malgré eux, échappent, par ce désespérant obstacle. Dans un si
grand accord, on dirait un combat. Des baleiniers prétendent avoir vu ce
spectacle unique. Les amants, d'un brûlant transport, par instants, dresses
et debout, comme les deux tours de Notre-Dame, gémissant de leurs bras trop
courts, entreprenaient de s'embrasser. Ils retombaient d'un poids immense . . .
L'ours et l'homme fuyaient épouvantés de leurs soupirs.

Michelet, *La Mer*, pages 240–42

So intense and poetic is this passage from Michelet it would
be wrong to tone it down with a translation.

Those days of intense sunshine and oppressive stillness when
a thick sultry heat weighs on the ocean – it occurred to me
these might be the rare moments when whales return in their
physiological memory to their terrestrial origins. To do this
they have to concentrate so intensely and completely that they
fall into a deep sleep which gives an appearance of death: and
thus floating on the surface, like blind, polished stumps, they
somehow remember, as though in a dream, a distant, distant

past when their clumsy fins were dry limbs capable of gestures, greetings, caresses, races through the grass amid tall flowers and ferns, on an earth that was a magma of elements still in search of a combination, an idea.

The whalemen of the Azores will tell you that when an adult whale is harpooned at a distance of five or six miles from another, the latter, even if in this state of apparent death, will wake with a start and flee in fear. The whales hunted in the Azores are mainly sperm whales.

Sperm Whale. This whale, among the English of old vaguely known as the Trumpa Whale, and the Physeter Whale and the Anvil Headed Whale, is the present Cachalot of the French, and the Pottfisch of the Germans, and the Macrocephalus of the Long Words. He is, without doubt, the largest inhabitant of the globe; the most formidable of all whales to encounter; the most majestic in aspect; and lastly, by far most valuable in commerce; he being the only creature from which that valuable substance, spermaceti, is obtained. All his peculiarities will, in many other places, be enlarged upon. It is chiefly with his name that I now have to do. Philologically considered, it is absurd. Some centuries ago, when the Sperm Whale was almost wholly unknown in his own proper individuality, and when his oil was only accidentally obtained from the stranded fish; in those days spermaceti, it would seem, was popularly supposed to be derived from a creature identical with the one then known in England as Greenland or Right Whale. It was the idea also, that this same spermaceti was that quickening humor of the Greenland Whale which the first syllable of the word literally expresses. In those times, also, spermaceti was exceedingly scarce, not being used for light, but only as an ointment and medicament. It was only to be had from the druggists as you nowadays buy an ounce of rhubarb. When, as I opine, in the course of time, the true nature of spermaceti became known its original name was still retained by the dealers; no doubt to enhance its value by a notion so strangely significant of its scarcity.

Melville, *Moby-Dick*, chapter XXXII

Sperm whales are great whales which live in areas of both hemispheres where the water temperature is fairly high. There are important differences between their physiology and that of other whales: the whalebones, which fortify the mouth of the latter and which are used to grind up small elements of food, are replaced in the sperm whale by sturdy teeth firmly inserted in the lower jaw and capable of snapping a large prey; the head, an enormous mass which ends vertically like the prow of a ship, accounts for a third of the whole body. These anatomical differences between the two groups of whales assign them to distinct territories: other whales find the thick banks of microscopic organisms they feed on mainly in the cold waters of the polar regions, where they absorb this food with the same naturalness with which we breathe; the sperm whale, on the other hand, mainly feeds on cephalopods which flourish in temperate waters. There are also important differences in the way these giant whales behave, differences which whalemen have learnt to recognize to perfection in the interests of their own safety. While other whales are peaceful animals, the older male sperm whale, like the boar, lives alone and will both defend and avenge himself. Having wounded the creature with their harpoons, many whaleboats have been snatched between the jaws of these giants and then crushed to pieces; and many crews have perished in the hunt.

Albert I, Prince of Monaco, *La Carrière d'un navigateur*, pages 277–78

No small number of these whaling seamen belong to the Azores, where the outward bound Nantucket whalers frequently touch to augment their crews from the hardy peasants of those rocky shores . . . How it is, there is no telling, but Islanders seem to make the best whalemen.

Melville, *Moby Dick*, chapter XXVII

The island of Pico is a volcanic cone which rises sheer from the ocean: it is no more and no less than a high rocky mountain resting on the water. There are three villages: Madalena, São Roque and Lajes; the rest is lava rock on which are dotted meagre vineyards and a few wild pineapples. The small ferry ties up at the landing stage in Madalena. It's Sunday and many families are taking trips to the nearby islands with baskets and bundles. The baskets are overflowing with pineapples, bananas, bottles of wine, fish. In Lajes there is a small whale museum I want to see. But since it's not a workday the bus isn't running very often and Lajes is forty kilometres away at the other end of the island. I sit patiently on a bench under a palm in front of the strange church that stands in the little *praça*. I planned to take a swim, it's a fine day and the temperature is pleasant. But on the ferry they told me to be careful, there's a dead whale near the rocks and the sea is full of sharks.

After a long wait in the midday heat I see a taxi which, having set down a passenger by the harbor, is turning back. The driver offers me a free ride to Lajes, because he has just made the trip and is going home, and the price his passenger paid included the return trip and he doesn't want any money he doesn't deserve. There are only two taxis in Lajes, he tells me with a satisfied look, his and his cousin's. Pico's only road runs along the cliffs with bends and potholes above a foaming sea. It's a narrow, bumpy road crossing a grim stony landscape, with just the occasional isolated village, dominated by an incongruously large eighteenth-century monastery and an imposing *padrão* – the stone monument that Portuguese sailors used to set up wherever they landed as a sign of their king's sovereignty.

The whale museum is in the main street on the first floor of a handsome renovated townhouse. My guide is a youngster with a vaguely half-witted air and a hackneyed, formal way of talking. What interests me most are the pieces of whale ivory which the whalemen used to carve, and then the ship's logs and some archaic tools of bizarre design. Along one wall are some old photographs. One bears the caption: *Lajes, 25 de Dezembro 1919.* Heaven knows how they managed to drag the sperm whale as far as the church. It must have taken quite a few pairs of oxen. It's a frighteningly huge sperm whale, it seems incredible. Six or seven young boys have climbed up onto its head: they've placed a ladder against the front of the head and are waving caps and handkerchiefs on top. The whalemen are lined up in the foreground with a proud, satisfied air. Three of them are wearing woolen bobble caps, one has an oilskin hat shaped like a fireman's. They are all barefoot, only one has boots, he must be the master. I imagine they then left the photograph, took off their caps and went into church, as if it were the most natural thing in the world to leave a whale in the square outside. Thus they spent Christmas day on Pico in 1919.

As I come out of the museum, a surprise awaits me. From the end of the street, still deserted, appears a band. They are old men and boys dressed in white with sailor's caps, their brass buttons brightly polished and winking in the sun. They're playing a melancholy air, a waltz it seems, and they play it beautifully. In front of them walks a little girl holding a staff on the end of which two bread rolls and a dove made of sugar have been skewered. I follow the little procession in their lonely parade along the main street as far as a house with blue windows. The band arranges itself in a semicircle and strikes up a dashing march. A window opens and an old man with a distinguished look to him greets them, leaning out, smiling. He disappears, then reappears a moment later on the doorstep. He is met with a short burst of applause, a hand-shake from the bandleader, a kiss from the little girl. Obviously this is a homage, though to whom or what I don't know, and there wouldn't be much sense in asking. The very short ceremony is over, the band rearranges itself into two lines, but instead of turning back they set off toward the sea which is right there at the bottom of the street. They start playing again and I follow them. When they reach the sea they sit on the rocks, put their instruments down on the ground and light up cigarettes. They chat and look at the sea. They're enjoying their Sunday. The girl has left her staff leaning against a lamp-post and is playing with a friend her own age. From the other end of the village the bus honks its horn, because at six it will be making its only trip to Madalena, and right now it's five to.

There are two sorts of whalemen in the Azores. The first come from the United States on small schooners of around a hundred tons. They look like pirate crews, because of the motley of races they include: negroes, Malays, Chinese, and indefinable cosmopolitan crosses of this or that, are all mixed up with deserters and rascals using the ocean as a means of escape from the justice of men. An enormous boiler takes up the centre of the schooner; it is here that the chunks of lubber cut from the captured sperm whale, which is tied to scaffolding beside the ship's hull, are transformed into oil using an infernal cooking process constantly disturbed by the pitch and roll of the boat: meanwhile coils of sickening smoke wreath all about. And when the sea is rough what a wild spectacle it becomes! Rather than give up the fruits of prey heroically snatched from the belly of the Ocean, these men prefer to put their lives in jeopardy. To double the ropes holding the whale to the scaffolding, a number of men will risk their lives climbing out on that enormous oily mass awash with rushing water, its great bulk tossed about by the waves and threatening to smash the hull of the schooner to pieces. Having doubled the ropes they will hang on, prolonging the risk to the point where it is no longer tolerable. Then they cut the hawsers and the whole crew shouts violent, angry imprecations at the carcass as it drifts off on the waves, leaving only a terrible stench where before it had inspired dreams of riches.

The other group of whalemen is made up of people more similar to common mortals. They are the fishermen of the islands, or even adventurous farmers, and sometimes simple emigrants who have come back to their own country, their souls tempered by other storms in the Americas. Ten of them will get together to make the crews for two whaling boats belonging to a tiny company with a capital of around thirty thousand francs. A third of the profits go to the shareholders, the other two thirds are divided equally between members of the crews. The whaling sloops are admirably built for speed and fitted with sails, oars, paddles, an ordinary rudder and an oar rudder. The hunting tools include several harpoons (their points carefully protected in cases), a number of fairly sharp steel lances, and five or six hundred metres of rope arranged in spirals inside baskets from which it runs forward through an upright fork on the prow of the boat.

These small boats lie in wait, concealed on small beaches or in the rocky bays of these inhospitable little islands. From a highpoint on the island a look-out constantly scans the sea the way a topman does on a ship; and when that column of watery stream the sperm whale blows out from his spiracle is sighted, the look-out musters the whalemen with an agreed signal. In a few minutes the boats have

taken to the sea and are heading towards the place where the drama
will be consummated.

Albert I, Prince of Monaco, *La Carrière d'un navigateur*, pages 280–83

From a Code of Regulations

I *Concerning the Whales*

Art. 1. These regulations are valid for the hunting of those whales
indicated below when hunting is carried out in the territorial waters
of Portugal and of the islands over which Portugal holds sovereignty:

Sperm whale, *Physeter catodon* (Linnaeus)
Common Whale, *Baloenoptera physalus* (Linnaeus)
Blue Whale, *Baloenoptera musculus* (Linnaeus)
Dwarf Whale, *Baloenoptera acustorostrata* (Linnaeus)
Hump-backed Whale or "Ampebeque," *Megaptera nodosa*
    (Linnaeus)

II *Concerning the Boats*

Art. 2. The craft used in the hunt shall be as follows:

a) *Whaling sloops.* Boats without decks, propelled by oar or sail,
used in the hunt, that is to harpoon or kill the whales.

b) *Launches.* Mechanically propelled boats used to assist the whaling sloops by towing them and the whales killed. When necessary and within the terms of these regulations, such boats may be used in the hunt itself to surround and harpoon the whales.

Art. 44. The dimensions of whaling sloops are fixed by law as follows: length, from 10 to 11.5 metres; width, from 1.8 to 1.95 metres.

Art. 45. The launches must have a weight of at least 4 tons and a speed of at least 8 knots.

Art. 51. In addition to such tools and equipment as are necessary for the hunt, all whaling boats must carry the following items on board: an axe to cut the harpoon rope if this should be necessary; three flags, one white, one blue, one red; a box of biscuits; a container with fresh water; three Holmes luminous torches.

III Concerning the Conduct of the Hunt

Art. 54. It is expressly forbidden to hunt whales with less than two boats.

Art. 55. It is forbidden to throw the harpoon when the boats are at such a distance from each other as not to be able to offer mutual assistance in the event of an accident.

Art. 56. In the event of an accident, all boats in the vicinity must assist those in difficulty, even if this means breaking off the hunt.

Art. 57. If a member of the crew should fall overboard during the hunt, the master of the boat involved will break off all hunting activity, cutting the harpoon rope if necessary, and will attend to the recovery of the man overboard to the exclusion of all else.

Art. 57a. If a boat captained by another master is present at the place where the accident occurs, this boat cannot refuse the necessary assistance.

Art. 57b. If the man overboard is the master, command will pass to the harpooneer, who must then follow the regulation described at Art. 57.

Art. 61. The direction of the hunt will be decided by the senior of the two masters, except where prior agreement to the contrary has been declared.

Art. 64. In the event of dead or dying whales being found out at sea or along the coast, those who find them must immediately inform the maritime authorities who will have the responsibility of proceeding to verify the report and to remove any harpoons. The finder of the whale will have the right to remuneration which will be paid under the terms of Art. 685 of the Commercial Code.

Art. 66. It is expressly forbidden to throw loose harpoons (that is, not secured to the boat with a rope) at a whale, whatever the circumstances. Anyone who does so does not establish any right over the whale harpooned.

Art. 68. No boat shall, without authorization, cut the ropes of other boats, unless forced to do so to preserve their own safety.

Art. 69. Harpoons, ropes, registration numbers, etc., found on a whale by other boats shall be returned to their rightful owners, nor does returning such items give any right to remuneration or indemnity.

Art. 70. It is forbidden to harpoon or kill whales of the Balaena species, commonly known as *French whales*.

Art. 71. It is forbidden to harpoon or kill female whales surprised while suckling their young, or young whales still at suckling age.

Art. 72. In order to preserve the species and better exploit hunting activities, it will be the responsibility of the Minister for the Sea to establish the sizes of the whales which may be caught and the periods of close season, to set quotas for the number of whales which may be hunted, and to introduce any other restrictive measures considered necessary.

Art. 73. The capture of whales for scientific purposes may be undertaken only after obtaining ministerial authorization.

Art. 74. It is expressly forbidden to hunt whales for sport.

"Regulations Governing the Hunting of Whales," published in the *Diário do Governo*, 19.5.54 and still in force

On the first Sunday in August the whalemen hold their annual festival in Horta. They line up their freshly painted boats in Porto Pim bay, the bell briefly rings out two hoarse clangs, the priest forms and climbs up to the promontory dominating the bay, where stands the chapel of Nossa Senhora da Guia. Behind the priest walk the women and children, with the whalemen bringing up the rear, each with his harpoon on his shoulder. They are very contrite and dressed in black. They all go into the chapel to hear Mass, leaving their harpoons standing against the wall outside, one next to the other, the way people elsewhere park their bicycles.

The harbor office is closed, but Senhor Chaves invites me in just the same. He is a distinguished, polite man with an open, slightly ironic smile and the blue eyes of some Flemish ancestor. There are hardly any left, he tells me, I don't think it'll be easy to find a boat. I ask if he means sperm whales and he laughs, amused. No, whalemen, he specifies, they've all emigrated to America, everybody in the Azores emigrates to America, the Azores are deserted, haven't you noticed? Yes, of course I have, I say, I'm sorry. Why? he asks. It's an embarrassing question. Because I like the Azores, I reply without much logic. So you'll like them even more deserted, he objects. And then he smiles as if to apologize for having been brusque. In any event, you see about getting yourself some life insurance, he concludes, otherwise I can't give you a permit. As for getting you on board, I'll sort that out, I'll speak to António José, who may be going out tomorrow, it seems there's a herd on the way. But I can't promise you a permit for more than two days.

A Hunt

It's a herd of six or seven, Carlos Eugénio tells me, his satisfied smile showing off such a brilliant set of false teeth it occurs to me he might have carved them himself from whale ivory. Carlos Eugénio is seventy, agile and still youthful, and he is *mestre baleeiro*, which, literally translated, means "master whaler," though in reality he is captain of this little crew and has absolute authority over every aspect of the hunt. The motor launch leading the expedition is his own, an old boat about ten metres long, which he maneuvers with deftness and nonchalance, and without any hurry either. In any event, he tells me, the whales are splashing about, they won't run away. The radio is on so as to keep in contact with the lookout based on a lighthouse on the island; a monotonous and it seems to me slightly ironic voice thus guides us on our way. "A little to the right, Maria Manuela," says the grating voice, "you're going all over the place." *Maria Manuela* is the name of the boat. Carlos Eugénio makes a gesture of annoyance, but still laughing, then he turns to the sailor who is riding with us, a lean, alert man, a boy almost, with constantly moving eyes and a dark complexion. We'll manage on our own, he decides, and turns the radio off. The sailor climbs nimbly up the boat's only mast and perches on the crosspiece at the top, wrapping his legs around. He too points to the right. For a moment I think he's sighted them, but I don't know the whaleman's sign language. Carlos Eugénio explains that an open hand with the index finger pointing upward means "whales in sight," and that wasn't the gesture our lookout made.

I turn to glance at the sloop we are towing. The whalemen are relaxed, laughing and talking together, though I can't make out what they're saying. They look as though they're out on a pleasure cruise. There are six of them and they're sitting on planks laid across the boat. The harpooner is standing up, though, and appears to be following our lookout's gestures with attention: he has a huge paunch and a thick beard, young, he can't be more than thirty. I've heard they call him Chá Preto, Black Tea, and that he works as a docker in the port in Horta. He belongs to the whaling cooperative in Faial, and they tell me he's an exceptionally skilled harpooner.

I don't notice the whale until we're barely three hundred metres: a column of water rises against the blue as when some pipe springs a leak in the road of a big city. Carlos Eugénio has turned off the engine and only our momentum takes us drifting on towards that black shape lying like an enormous bowler hat on the water. In the sloop the whalemen are silently preparing for the attack: they are calm, quick, resolute, they know the motions they have to go through by heart. They row with powerful, well-spaced strokes, and in a flash they are far away. They go round in a wide circle, approaching the whale from the front so as to avoid the tail, and because if they approached from the sides they would be in sight of its eyes. When they are a hundred metres off they draw their oars into the boat and raise a small triangular sail. Everybody adjusts sail and ropes: only the harpooner is immobile on the point of the prow: standing, one leg bent forward, the harpoon lying in his hand as if he were measuring its weight. He concentrates, hanging on for the right moment, the moment when the boat will be near enough for him to strike a vital point, but far enough away not to be caught by a lash of the wounded whale's tail. Everything happens with amazing speed in just a few seconds. The boat makes a sudden turn while the harpoon is still curving through the air. The instrument of death isn't flung from above downwards, as I had expected, but upwards, like a javelin, and it is the sheer weight of the iron and the speed of the thing as it falls that transforms it into a deadly missile. When the enormous tail rises to whip first the air then the water, the sloop is already far away. The oarsmen are rowing again, furiously, and a strange play of ropes, which until now was going on underwater so that I hadn't seen it, suddenly becomes visible and I realize that our launch is connected to the harpoon too, while the whaling sloop has jettisoned its own rope. From a straw basket placed in a well in the middle of the launch, a thick rope begins to unwind, sizzling as it rushes through a fork on the bow; the young deckhand pours a bucket of water over it to cool it and prevent it snapping from the friction. Then the rope tightens and we set off with a jerk, a leap, following the wounded whale as it flees. Carlos Eugénio holds the helm and chews the stub of a cigarette; the sailor with the boyish face watches the sperm whale's movements with a worried expression. In his hand he holds a small sharp axe ready to cut the rope if the whale should go down, since it would drag us with it underwater. But the breathless rush doesn't last long. We've hardly gone a kilometre when the whale stops dead, apparently exhausted, and Carlos Eugénio has to put the launch into reverse to stop the momentum from taking us on top of the immobile animal. He struck well, he says with satisfaction, showing off his brilliant false teeth. As if in confirmation of his comment, the whale, whistling, raises his head right out of the water and breathes; and the jet that hisses up into the air is red with blood. A pool of vermilion spreads across the sea and the breeze carries a spray of red drops as far as our boat, spotting faces and clothes. The whaling sloop has drawn up against the launch: Chá Petro throws his tools up on deck and climbs up himself with an agility truly surprising for a man of his build. I gather that he wants to go on to the next stage of the attack, the lance, but the *mestre* seems not to agree. There follows some excited confabulation, which the sailor with the boyish face keeps out of. Then Chá Petro obviously gets his way; he stands on the prow and assumes his javelin-throwing stance, having swapped the harpoon for a weapon of the same size but with an extremely sharp head in an elongated heart shape, like a halberd. Carlos Eugénio moves forward with the engine on minimum, and the boat starts over to where the whale is breathing, immobile in a pool of blood, restless tail spasmodically slapping the water. This time the deadly weapon is thrown downwards; hurled on a slant, it penetrates the soft flesh as if it were butter. A dive: the great mass disappears, writhing underwater. Then the tail appears again, powerless, pitiful, like a black sail. And finally the huge head emerges and I hear the deathcry, a sharp wail, almost a whistle, shrill, agonizing, unbearable.

The whale is dead and lies motionless on the water. The coagulated blood forms a bank that looks like coral. I hadn't realized the day was almost over, and dusk surprises me. The whole crew are busy organizing the towing. Working quickly, they punch a hole in the tail fin and thread through a rope with a stick to lock it. We are more than eighteen miles out to sea, Carlos Eugénio tells me; it will take all night to get back, the sperm whale weighs around thirty tons and the launch will have to go very slowly. In a strange marine rope party led by the launch and with the whale bringing up the rear, we head towards the island of Pico and the factory of São Roque. In the middle is the sloop with the whalemen, and Carlos Eugénio suggests I join them so as to be able to get a little rest: under enormous strain, the launch's engine is making an infernal racket and sleep would be impossible. The two boats draw alongside each other and Carlos Eugénio leaves the launch with me, handing over the helm to the young sailor and two oarsmen who take our place. The whalemen set up a makeshift bed for me near the tiller; night has fallen and two oil lanterns have been lit on the sloop. The fishermen are exhausted, their faces strained and serious, tinted yellow in the light from the lanterns. They hoist the sail so as not to be a dead weight increasing the strain on the launch, then lie any-old-how across the planks and fall into a deep sleep. Chá Preto sleeps on his back, paunch up, and snores loudly. Carlos Eugénio offers me a cigarette and talks to me about his two children, who have emigrated to America and whom he hasn't seen for six years. They came back just once, he tells me, maybe they'll come again next summer. They'd like me to go to them, but I want to die here, at home. He smokes slowly and watches the sky, the stars. What about you, though, why did you want to come with us today, he asks me, out of simple curiosity? I hesitate, thinking how to answer: I'd like to tell him the truth, but am held back by the fear that this might offend. I let a hand dangle in the water. If I stretched out my arm I could almost touch the enormous fin of the animal we're towing. Perhaps you're both a dying breed, I finally say softly, you people and the whales, I think that's why I came. Probably he's already asleep, he doesn't answer; though the coal of his cigarette still burns between his fingers. The sail slaps sombrely; motionless in sleep, the bodies of the whalemen are small dark heaps and the sloop slides over the water like a ghost.

The Woman of Porto Pim

A Story

I sing every evening, because that's what I'm paid to do, but the songs you heard were *pesinhos* and *sapateiras* for the tourists and for those Americans over there laughing at the back. They'll get up and stagger off soon. My real songs are *chamaritas*, just four of them, because I don't have a big repertoire and then I'm getting on, and I smoke a lot, my voice is hoarse. I have to wear this *balandrau*, the traditional old Azores costume, because Americans like things to be picturesque, then they go back to Texas and say how they went to a tavern on a godforsaken island where there was an old man dressed in an ancient cloak singing his people's folksongs. They want the *viola de arame*, which has this proud, melancholy sound, and I sing them sugary *modinhas*, with the same rhyme all the time, but it doesn't matter because they don't understand, and then as you can see, they're drinking gin and tonics. But what about you, though, what are you after, coming here every evening? You're curious and you're looking for something different, because this is the second time you've offered me a drink, you order *cheiro* wine as if you were one of us, you're a foreigner and you pretend to speak like us, but you don't drink much and then you don't say anything either, you wait for me to speak. You said you were a writer, and that maybe your job was something like mine. All books are stupid, there's never much truth in them, still I've read a lot over the last thirty years, I haven't had much else to do, Italian books too, all in translation of course. The one I liked most was called *Canaviais no vento*, by someone called Deledda, do you know it? And then you're young and you have an eye for the women, I saw the way you were looking at that beautiful woman with the long neck, you've been watching her all evening, I don't know if she's your girlfriend, she was looking at you too, and maybe you'll find it strange but all this has reawakened something in me, it must be because I've had too much to drink.

I've always done things to excess in life, a road that leads to perdition, but if you're born like that you can't do anything about it.

In front of our house there was an *atafona*, that's what they're called on this island, a sort of wheel for drawing up water that turned round and round, they don't exist any more, I'm talking about years and years ago, before you were even born. If I think of it now, I can still hear it creaking, it's one of the childhood sounds that have stuck in my memory, my mother would send me with a pitcher to get some water and to make it less tiring I used to sing a lullaby as I pushed and sometimes I really would fall asleep. Beyond the water wheel there was a low whitewashed wall and then a sheer drop down to the sea. There were three of us children and I was the youngest. My father was a slow man, he used to weigh his words and gestures and his eyes were so clear they looked like water. His boat was called *Madrugada*, which was also my mother's maiden name. My father was a whaleman, like his father before him, but in the seasons when there were no whales, he used to fish for moray eels, and we went with him, and our mother too. People don't do it now, but when I was a child there was a ritual that was part of going fishing. You catch morays in the evening, with a waxing moon, and to call them there was a song which had no words: it was a song, a tune, that started low and languid, then turned shrill. I never heard a song so sorrowful, it sounded like it was coming from the bottom of the sea, or from lost souls in the night, a song as old as our islands. Nobody knows it any more, it's been lost, and maybe it's better that way, since there was a curse in it, or a destiny, like a spell. My father went out with the boat, it was dark, he moved the oars softly, dipping them in vertically so as not to make any noise, and the rest of us, my brothers and my mother, would sit on the rocks and start to sing. Sometimes the others would keep quiet, they wanted me to call the eels, because they said my voice was more melodious than anybody else's and the morays couldn't resist it. I don't believe my voice was any better than theirs: they wanted me to sing on my own because I was the youngest and people used to say that the eels liked clear voices. Perhaps it was just superstition and there was nothing in it, but that hardly matters.

Then we grew up and my mother died. My father became more taciturn and sometimes, at night, he would sit on the wall by the cliffs and look at the sea. By now we only went out after whales; we three boys were big and strong and Father gave us the harpoons and the lances, since he was getting too old. Then one day my brothers left. The second oldest went to America, he only told us the day he left, I went to the harbour to see him off, my father didn't come. The other went to be a truck driver on the mainland, he was always laughing and he'd always loved the sound of engines; when the army man came to tell us about the accident I was at home alone and I told my father over supper.

We two still went out whaling. It was more difficult now, we had to take on casual labour for the day, because you can't go out with less than five, then my father would have liked me to get married, because a home without a woman isn't a real home. But I was twenty-five and I liked playing at love; every Sunday I'd go down to the harbour and get a new girlfriend. It was wartime in Europe and there were lots of people passing through the Azores. Every day a ship would moor here or on another island, and in Porto Pim you could hear all kinds of languages.

I met her one Sunday in the harbour. She was wearing

white, her shoulders were bare and she had a lace cap. She looked as though she'd climbed out of a painting, not from one of those ships full of people fleeing to the Americas. I looked at her a long time and she looked at me too. It's strange how love can find a way through to you. It got to me when I noticed two small wrinkles just forming round her eyes and I thought: she isn't that young. Maybe I thought like that because, being the boy I still was then, a mature woman seemed older to me than her real age. I only found out she wasn't much over thirty a lot later, when knowing her age would be of no use at all. I said good morning to her and asked if I could help her in any way. She pointed to the suitcase at her feet. Take it to the *Bote*, she said in my own language. The *Bote* is no place for a lady, I said. I'm not a lady, she answered, I'm the new owner.

Next Sunday I went down to town again. In those days the *Bote* was a strange kind of bar, not exactly a place for fishermen, and I'd only been there once before. I knew there were two private rooms at the back where rumour had it people gambled, and that the bar itself had a low ceiling, a large ornate mirror and tables made out of fig wood. The customers were all foreigners, they looked as though they were on holiday, while the truth was they spent all day spying on each other and pretending to come from countries they didn't really come from, and when they weren't spying they played cards. Faial was an incredible place in those days. Behind the bar was a Canadian called Denis, a short man with pointed sideburns who spoke Portuguese like someone from Cape Verde. I knew him because he came to the harbour on Saturdays to buy fish; you could eat at the *Bote* on Sunday evening. It was Denis who later taught me English.

I want to speak to the owner, I said. The owner doesn't come until after eight, he answered haughtily. I sat down at a table and ordered supper. She came in towards nine, there were other regulars around, she saw me and nodded vaguely, then sat in a corner with an old man with a white moustache. It was only then that I realised how beautiful she was, a beauty that made my temples burn. This was what had brought me there, but until then I hadn't really understood. And now, in the space of a moment, it all fell into place inside me so clearly it almost made me dizzy. I spent the evening staring at her, my temples resting on my fists, and when she went out I followed her at a distance. She walked with a light step, without turning;

she didn't seem to be worried about being followed. She went under the gate in the big wall of Porto Pim and began to go down to the bay. On the other side of the bay, where the promontory ends, isolated among the rocks, between a cane thicket and a palm tree, there's a stone house. Maybe you've already noticed it. It's abandoned now and the windows are in poor shape, there's something sinister about it; some day the roof will fall in, if it hasn't already. She lived there, but in those days it was a white house with blue panels over the doors and windows. She went in and closed the door and the light went out. I sat on a rock and waited; halfway through the night a window lit up, she looked out and I looked at her. The nights are quiet in Porto Pim, you only need to whisper in the dark to be heard far away. Let me in, I begged her. She closed the shutter and turned off the light. The moon was coming up in a veil of red, a summer moon. I felt a great longing, the water lapped around me, everything was so intense and so unattainable, and I remembered when I was a child, how at night I used to call the eels from the rocks: then an idea came to me, I couldn't resist, and I began to sing that song. I sang it very softly, like a lament, or a supplication, with a hand held to my ear to guide my voice. A few moments later the door opened and I went into the dark of the house and found myself in her arms. I'm called Yeborath, was all she said.

Do you know what betrayal is? Betrayal, real betrayal, is when you feel so ashamed you wish you were somebody else. I wished I'd been somebody else when I went to say goodbye to my father and his eyes followed me about as I wrapped my harpoon in oilskin and hung it on a nail in the kitchen, then slung the viola he'd given me for my twentieth birthday over my shoulder. I've decided to change jobs, I told him quickly, I'm going to sing in a bar in Porto Pim, I'll come and see you Saturdays. But I didn't go that Saturday, nor the Saturday after, and lying to myself I'd say I'd go and see him the next Saturday. So autumn came and the winter went, and I sang. I did other little jobs too, because sometimes customers would drink too much and to keep them on their feet or chase them off you needed a strong arm, which Denis didn't have. And then I listened to what the customers said while they pretended to be on holiday; it's easy to pick up people's secrets when you sing in a bar, and, as you see, it's easy to tell them too. She would wait for me in her house in Porto Pim and I didn't have to knock any more now. I asked her: Who are you? Where are you from? Why don't we leave these absurd people pretending to play cards? I want to be with you for ever. She laughed and left me to guess the reasons why she was living the way she was, and she said: Wait just a little longer and we'll leave together, you have to trust me, I can't tell you any more. Then she'd stand naked at the window, looking at the moon, and say: Sing me your eel song, but softly. And while I sang she'd ask me to make love to her, and I'd take her standing up, leaning against the windowsill, while she looked out into the night, as though waiting for something.

It happened on August 10. It was São Lourenço and the sky was full of shooting stars, I counted thirteen of them walking home. I found the door locked and I knocked. Then I knocked again louder, because there was a light on. She opened and stood in the doorway, but I pushed her aside. I'm going tomorrow, she said, the person I was waiting for has come back. She smiled, as if to thank me, and I don't know why but I thought she was thinking of my song. At the back of the room a figure moved. He was an old man and he was getting dressed. What's he want? he asked her in the language I now understood. He's drunk, she said; he was a whaler once but he gave up his harpoon for the viola, while you were away he worked as my servant. Send him away, said the man, without looking at me.

There was a pale light over Porto Pim. I went around the bay as if in one of those dreams where you suddenly find yourself at the other end of the landscape. I didn't think of anything, because I didn't want to think. My father's house was dark, since he went to bed early. But he wouldn't sleep, he'd lie still in the dark the way old people often do, as if that were a kind of sleep. I went in without lighting the lamp, but he heard me. You're back, he murmured. I went to the far wall and took my harpoon off the hook. I found my way in the moonlight. You can't go after whales at this time of night, he said from his bunk. It's an eel, I said. I don't know if he understood what I meant, but he didn't object, or get up. I think he lifted a hand to wave me goodbye, but maybe it was my imagination or the play of shadows in the half dark. I never saw him again. He died long before I'd done my time. I've never seen my brother again either. Last year I got a photo of him, a fat man with white hair surrounded by a group of strangers who must be his sons and daughters-in-law, sitting on the veranda of a wooden house, and the colours are too bright, like in a postcard. He said if I wanted to go and live with him, there was work there for everybody and life was easy. That almost made me laugh. What could it mean, an easy life, when your life is already over?

And if you stay a bit longer and my voice doesn't give out, I'll sing you the song that decided the destiny of this life of mine. I haven't sung it for thirty years and maybe my voice isn't up to it. I don't know why I'm offering, I'll dedicate it to that woman with the long neck, and to the power a face has to surface again in another's, maybe that's what's touched a chord. And to you, young Italian, coming here every evening, I can see you're hungry for true stories to turn them into paper, so I'll make you a present of this story you've heard. You can even write down the name of the man who told it to you, but not the name they know me by in this bar, which is a name for tourists passing through. Write that this is the true story of Lucas Eduino who killed the woman he'd thought was his, with a harpoon, in Porto Pim.

Oh, there was just one thing she hadn't lied to me about; I found out at the trial. She really was called Yeborath. If that's important at all.

Postscript

A Whale's View of Man

Always so feverish, and with those long limbs waving about. Not rounded at all, so they don't have the majesty of complete, rounded shapes sufficient unto themselves, but little moving heads where all their strange life seems to be concentrated. They arrive sliding across the sea, but not swimming, as if they were birds almost, and they bring death with frailty and graceful ferocity. They're silent for long periods, but then shout at each other with unexpected fury, a tangle of sounds that hardly vary and don't have the perfection of our basic cries: the call, the love cry, the death lament. And how pitiful their lovemaking must be: and bristly, brusque almost, immediate, without a soft covering of fat, made easy by their threadlike shape which excludes the heroic difficulties of union and the magnificent and tender efforts to achieve it.

They don't like water, they're afraid of it, and it's hard to understand why they bother with it. Like us they travel in herds, but they don't bring their females, one imagines they must be elsewhere, but always invisible. Sometimes they sing, but only for themselves, and their song isn't a call to others, but a sort of longing lament. They soon get tired and when evening falls they lie down on the little islands that take them about and perhaps fall asleep or watch the moon. They slide silently by and you realize they are sad.

Appendix

A Map, a Note, a Few Books

A Map

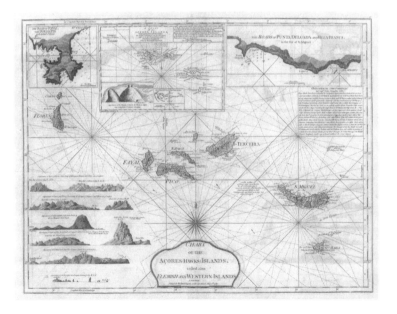

A Note

The Azores archipelago is situated in the middle of the Atlantic Ocean, about halfway between Europe and America, between latitudes 36°55' and 39°44'N and longitudes 25° to 31°W. It is composed of nine islands: Santa Maria, São Miguel, Terceira, Graciosa, São Jorge, Pico, Faial, Flores and Corvo. The archipelago stretches across a distance of around 600 km from NW to SE. The name Azores is the result of an error on the part of the first Portuguese sailors; they mistook for sparrow-hawks (in Portuguese, *açores*) what in fact were numerous kites which populate the islands.

Portuguese colonization began in 1432 and went on for the whole of the fifteenth century, though at the same time the Azores also became the home of a large number of Flemish colonists, this as a result of marriages which linked the Portuguese throne with Flanders. The Flemish colonists left a considerable mark, not just on the physical features of the inhabitants, but also on the islands' popular music and folklore in general. The soil is volcanic in origin. The rocky coasts are often made up of sheets of extremely hard lava, while in flatter areas there are stretches of pulverized pumice stone. The physical characteristics of the landscape show very clear signs of volcanic and seismic activity. As well as a whole series of minor volcanic phenomena (smokeholes, geysers, warm springs and mud swamps, etc.), there is an abundance of volcanic lakes which have taken over ancient craters, and the landscape is often broken by deep crevices scored out by the burning lava. The hinterland and the mountains have a savage and often gloomy beauty. The highest peak is Pico, which is 2,345 metres high and located on the island of the same name. Innumerable volcanic eruptions have been recorded: the most terrifying earthquakes took place in 1522, 1538, 1591, 1630, 1755, 1810, 1862, 1884, 1957. The effects of the 1978 earthquake, which hit the island of Terceira in particular, are clearly visible to any traveler stopping over in Angra. In the course of this incessant volcanic activity, the landscape of the Azores has been subjected to considerable change and countless little islands have surfaced and then disappeared. The most curious anecdote in this regard was told by an English sea captain, Tillard. In 1810, on board his warship, the *Sabrina*, Tillard witnessed the birth of a little island on which he had two men land with an English flag, claiming possession of the territory for the English crown and baptizing it Sabrina. But the day after, before lifting anchor, Captain Tillard was to find to his disappointment that the island of Sabrina had disappeared and the sea was as flat and calm as ever.

The climate of the Azores is mild, with abundant but brief rainfalls and very hot summers. Nature is luxuriant and there are countless species of plants. Typically Mediterranean flora, in which cedars, vines, orange trees and pines dominate, flourishes alongside tropical vegetation which includes pineapple trees, banana trees, passion fruit and a huge variety of flowers. Birds and butterflies abound, but there are no reptiles. Whale hunting, using the traditional methods described in this book, is now practiced only in Pico and Faial. In our century, the emigration of large numbers of people, for mainly economic reasons, has considerably depleted the archipelago's population. Corvo, Flores and Santa Maria are almost uninhabited.

A Few Books

ALBERT I, PRINCE OF MONACO, *La Carrière d'un navigateur*, Monaco, 1905 (with no publisher's name).

RAÚL BRANDÃO, *As Ilhas desconhecidas*, Bertrand, Rio-Paris, 1926.

JOSEPH AND HENRY BULLAR, *A Winter in the Azores and a Summer at the Furnas*, John van Voorst, London, 1841.

"DIÁRIO DE MISS NYE," in *Insulana*, vol. XXIX–XXX, Ponta Delgada, 1973–74.

J. MOUSINHO FIGUEIREDO, *Introdução ao estudo da indústria baleeira insular*, Astória, Lisbon, 1945.

GASPAR FRUTUOSO, *Saudades da Terra*, 6 vols., Lisbon, 1569–91 (a modern edition with updated orthography; Ponta Delgada, 1963–64).

JULES MICHELET, *La Mer*, Hachette, Paris, 1861.

ANTERO DE QUENTAL, *Sonetos*, Coimbra, 1861 (and countless later editions).

CAPTAIN JOSHUA SLOCUM, *Sailing Alone Around the World*, Rupert Hart-Davis, London, 1940 (first edition 1900).

BERNARD VENABLES, *Baleia! The Whalers of the Azores*, The Bodley Head, London-Sydney-Toronto, 1968.

archipelago books

is a not-for-profit literary press devoted to

promoting cross-cultural exchange through innovative

classic and contemporary international literature

www.archipelagobooks.org